REVENGE OF THE
MAN-EATING GERBILS

David Orme lives in Winchester and
is the author of a wide range of
poetry books, textbooks and picture
books for children. When he is not
writing he visits schools, performing
poetry, running workshops and
encouraging children and teachers to
enjoy poetry.

Woody lives in London and has been
illustrating children's books for the

REVENGE OF THE MAN-EATING GERBILS

Chosen by
David Orme

and illustrated by
Woody

01424

MACMILLAN CHILDREN'S BOOKS

First published 1999 by
Macmillan Children's Books
a division of Macmillan Publishers Ltd
25 Eccleston Place London SW1W 9NF
Basingstoke and Oxford
www.macmillan.co.uk

Associated companies throughout the world

ISBN 0 330 35487 6

3 5 7 9 8 6 4 2

A CIP catalogue record for this book is available from the British Library.

Typeset by Macmillan Children's Books
Printedand bound in Great Britain by Mackays of Chatham Plc, Kent

Contents

The Worm's Prelude 8
Tony Mitton

The Pong 10
John Mole

When Great-Grandmother Takes 12
Her False Teeth Out
Bernard Young

RIP Recipes 14
John Kitching

Bad Friday 16
John C. Desmond

Lost Property 18
Coral Rumble

Drinking the Dregs from 20
the Staffroom Cups
Paul Cookson

There's Nothing Quite Like 24
a Cowpat!
Andrew Collett

The Fishbone Voyage   26
Tony Mitton

Innoculation   28
Brian Moses

Blow Out   30
Dave Calder

Going One Better   33
Paul Cookson

Remains   35
John Kitching

Nursery Rhymes   37
Matt Simpson

Dinner on Elm Street   38
Michaela Morgan

Choosing Schools   41
Angi Holden

Fido Has Died, Oh   42
John Coldwell

Revenge of the Man-eating Gerbils   44
Mike Johnson

Archie   46
Angi Holden

Babies are so . . .   **48**
John Rice

Gnash   **49**
Dave Calder

My Mates   **50**
Gus Grenfell

Fresh on the Menu Tonight   **52**
Pat Leighton

Currant Bun Riddle   **54**
Andrew Collett

Rover   **56**
Wes Magee

Hug a Slug!   **58**
Ian Souter

Let's Face It   **59**
John Kitching

The Worm's Prelude

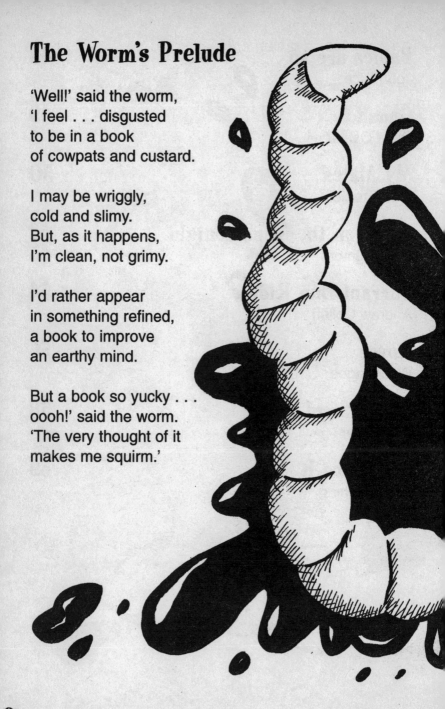

'Well!' said the worm,
'I feel . . . disgusted
to be in a book
of cowpats and custard.

I may be wriggly,
cold and slimy.
But, as it happens,
I'm clean, not grimy.

I'd rather appear
in something refined,
a book to improve
an earthy mind.

But a book so yucky . . .
oooh!' said the worm.
'The very thought of it
makes me squirm.'

The worm took a breath
and held its nose.
'Better get on with it,
I suppose.

Here goes . . .'

Tony Mitton

The Pong

It might have come from Peter,
It might have come from Dean,
But when they stood together
It was sort of in between.

It smelt a bit like armpits
It smelt a bit like feet,
And if either walked away
It was sort of incomplete.

John Mole

When Great-Grandmother Takes Her False Teeth Out

When Great-Grandmother takes
her false teeth out
we fear her rubbery grin.

When she unsticks
those two fat lips of hers
– what a cavern!
we're scared of falling in . . .

Deep down, in her stomach,
are all the extra-strong mints she's sucked
and the overcooked cabbage
and the sprouts and the occasional roast duck
and the spoonfuls of syrup she took
to ease that tickly cough
and the oceans of sweet milky tea
that she can't seem to get enough of;
and those little nips of rum she's partial to
were a puddle, then a pond, now a lake
and she has her very own Everest – a mountain
of biscuit and cream and cake;
and there's toast and marmalade and cornflakes
porridge and apples and plums
plus all the stuff we haven't thought of
swimming inside her tum.

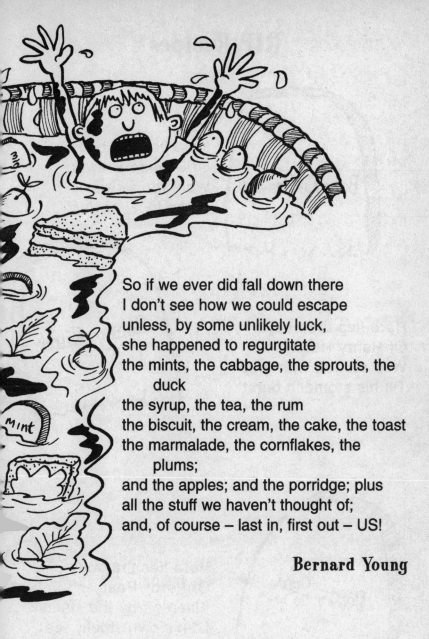

So if we ever did fall down there
I don't see how we could escape
unless, by some unlikely luck,
she happened to regurgitate
the mints, the cabbage, the sprouts, the
    duck
the syrup, the tea, the rum
the biscuit, the cream, the cake, the toast
the marmalade, the cornflakes, the
    plums;
and the apples; and the porridge; plus
all the stuff we haven't thought of;
and, of course – last in, first out – US!

Bernard Young

RIP Recipes

Here lies the body
Of Belinda Brewer:
Went for a swim
In the local sewer.

Here lies the body
Of Henry Hurst
Who stuffed with grub
Till his stomach burst

Here lies the body
Of Percy Peat,
Killed off by the stench
Of his own smelly feet.

Here lies the body
Of Wendy Wise.
She ate a mince pie
That was packed with
     flies.

Here lies the body
Of Harriet Hick,
Stuffed with chocolate.
Sick! Sick! Sick!

Here lies the body
Of Patrick Jones:
Ate a whole elephant,
Skin and bones.

John Kitching

Bad Friday

Lying, soaking up the warmth
he became aware
of an approaching fin
ploughing the surface.
Then the pain; his right leg
severed at the knee.
Panic as he tried to swim
but his arms refused.

A second strike gouged his midriff.
Gasping for air he swallowed.
Drowning in blood;
a pounding in his head
and a faint voice –
'Will you be much longer in there?'

John C. Desmond

Lost Property

(The Headteacher's Announcement)

'Hmm, hmm . . .

A sandwich has been spotted
In the corner of the hall,
Some say it has the odour
To anaesthetize us all:
It has crawled behind the benches,
Adding fluff balls to its grime,
And rolled under the wall-bars –
Must have been there for some time.

Miss Pope says, though she's not certain,
That she's seen it twice before;
Once sliding in the gym, then squashed
Underneath the library door.
And about a month ago, I've heard,
Mr Scott, our new caretaker,
Complained of mouldy, doughy smells
From behind a radiator.

If this over-active, agèd lunch,
Well-past its sell-by date,
Belongs to you then please act now
Before it is too late.
Lost property just cannot cope
With items that are squidgy,
Might I suggest unwanted food
Be returned home to your fridgy.

Hmm, hmm . . . Thank you'

Coral Rumble

Drinking the Dregs from the Staffroom Cups

Griff and me had a dare.
Who would be brave enough to . . .
drink all the dregs from the teacher's cups in the
    staffroom.

We stayed late last night,
waited till all the teachers had gone home
then crept into the staffroom.
What a mess! Paper, books, half-eaten sandwiches,
apple cores, yoghurt pots, banana skins, crisp
    crumbs . . .
chocolate wrappers, mouldy milk . . .
and our homework from last year.
Blimey! It was worse than my little brother's bedroom.

We collected all the cups onto one table.
Thirty-seven of them all together.
Some were more than half full.
All were cold and slimy with skin on the top.
Most were green and furry . . . different shades of green.
It looked like a science experiment.
I thought the green was mould.
Griff thought it was alien slime from Mr. Hooter's nose.
Several cups had cigarette ends in.
Others had floaty white lumps
which could have been congealed powdered milk, cheese
or chalkdust . . . or possibly all three.
At least one seemed to have been soup
judging by the unidentifiable blobs encrusted
        round the rim.
I thought I could see some croutons or
        breadcrumbs in there
somewhere but Griff thought differently . . .

He said the flaky bits were old Mr Raymond's
    dandruff.

Anyway, the dare was . . .
to drink as many as possible without stopping.
We looked at each other, held our noses, took a
    deep breath
– then had a much better idea
and emptied all the dregs in the teacher's
    teapot,
the big brown one that's always there.
We mixed them all up with a big stick,
added a bit of washing-up liquid, a slice of
    school gravy,
several chewed up fingernails, a tube of my spot
    cream,
a quick spray of Ralgex, four dead flies from the
    sink,
my used tissue and one of Griff's football socks
then put the top back on.

Today, outside the staffroom,
we heard the teachers talking as they ran to the toilets.
They said how clean their cups were for a change
and how the tea tasted much nicer than usual.

Paul Cookson

There's Nothing Quite Like a Cowpat!

There's nothing quite like a cowpat
they're so easy to spot;
some are cold and crunchy
and others steaming hot.

Some will smell of filthy things
like sick or sweaty feet,
but others will whiff of daffodils
and seem good enough to eat.

Some will look like doughnut rings
without the jam inside,
some will make you slip and fall
and others will make you slide.

Some will sit all alone
some will line in pairs,
some will be completely bald
whilst others might have hairs.

Some will have a smiley face
some even have a name,
for when it comes to cowpats
then no two are quite the same!

ndrew Collett

The Fishbone Voyage

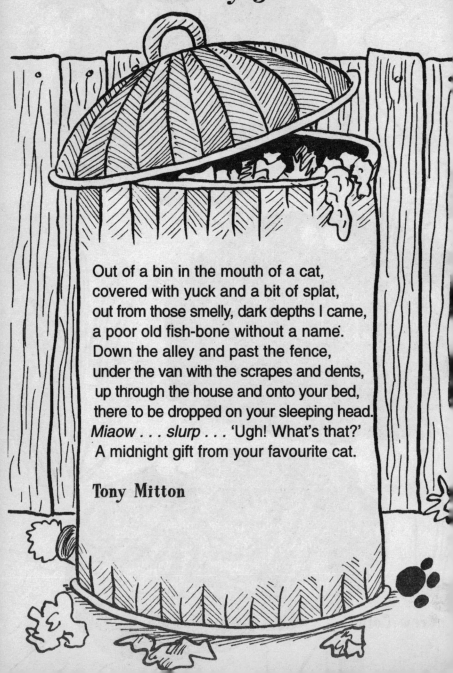

Out of a bin in the mouth of a cat,
covered with yuck and a bit of splat,
out from those smelly, dark depths I came,
a poor old fish-bone without a name.
Down the alley and past the fence,
under the van with the scrapes and dents,
up through the house and onto your bed,
there to be dropped on your sleeping head.
Miaow . . . slurp . . . 'Ugh! What's that?'
A midnight gift from your favourite cat.

Tony Mitton

INNOCULATION

When the notes came round
and I read the terrible word,
INNOCULATION,
I knew just what to expect.

I'd heard from Ben's brother last year,
how he couldn't move his arm.
He wore it in a sling for weeks.
It went sceptic, where they rammed it in,
came up in a lump – the needle
was huge – like a bicycle pump.

It needed three nurses to hold him down.
He'd been gagged, blindfolded
while the needle jiggered and jumped around
like a road drill,
and all the while he'd howled.

Dad didn't help either –
'In the army,' he said, 'they lined you up –
thump, thump, thump!
When it got to you
the needle was blunt.'

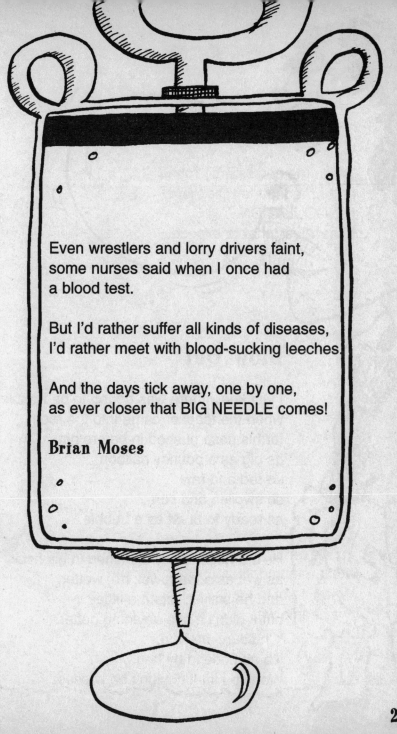

Even wrestlers and lorry drivers faint,
some nurses said when I once had
a blood test.

But I'd rather suffer all kinds of diseases,
I'd rather meet with blood-sucking leeches.

And the days tick away, one by one,
as ever closer that BIG NEEDLE comes!

Brian Moses

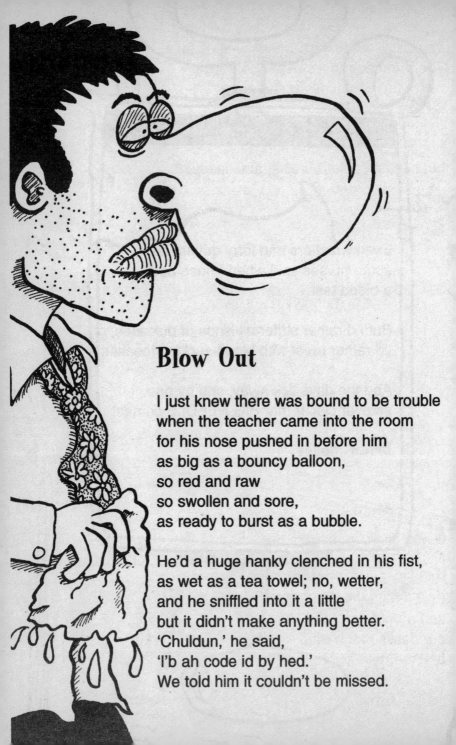

Blow Out

I just knew there was bound to be trouble
when the teacher came into the room
for his nose pushed in before him
as big as a bouncy balloon,
so red and raw
so swollen and sore,
as ready to burst as a bubble.

He'd a huge hanky clenched in his fist,
as wet as a tea towel; no, wetter,
and he sniffled into it a little
but it didn't make anything better.
'Chuldun,' he said,
'I'b ah code id by hed.'
We told him it couldn't be missed.

You could tell that he wasn't well pleased.
Then he opened his mouth, but what
he meant to say never came out
for his face twisted up in a knot
and he snuffled and snorted
he struggled and fought it
but he just couldn't stop it, and sneezed.

We watched as if caught in a dream
as the vast twitching lump of his nose
swung back and blasted straight at us
with the roar of twenty tornadoes:
he blew out with a boom
that rocked the whole room –
I could hardly hear myself scream.

It was all in the papers next day:
NOSE EXPLODES – DISASTER STRIKES SCHOOL
KILLER SNEEZE WIPES TEACHER OUT
FIVE STILL IN HOSPITAL
and a photo showed
our desks in the road
and the hole where the
    wall blew away.

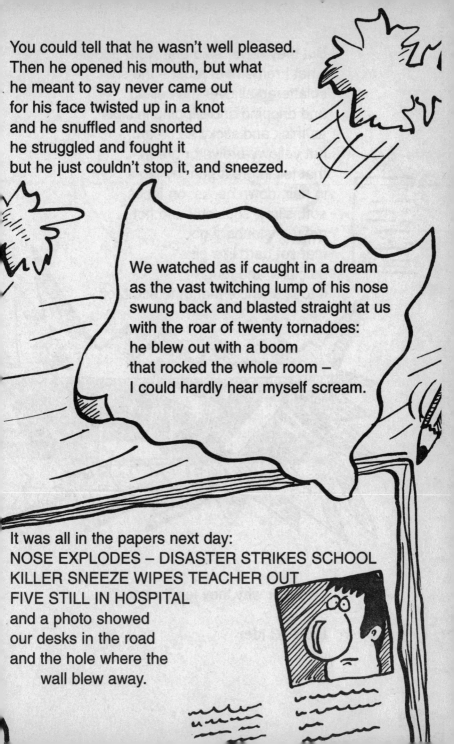

But they never said one word about
what I remember most – the snot
splattered all over the ceiling
and dripping and slipping in clots
as thick and sticky as cream,
but yellowy-brown or green;
that fell in great gungey blots
in hair, down necks, on faces,
soft, slimy, squelchy and hot
gobs of slobbery goo
that set hard like glue
so clarty and tough
it took a whole month to scrub off –

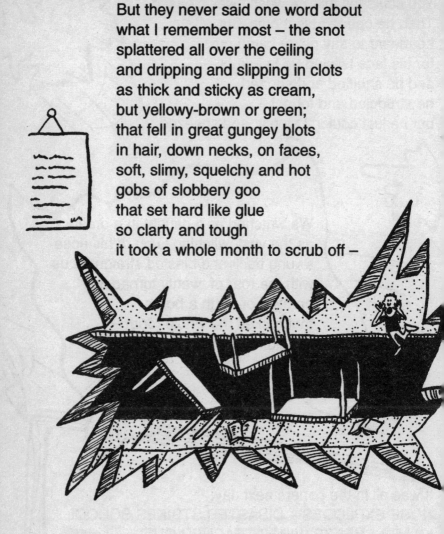

I wonder why they left that out?

Dave Calder

Going One Better

Sister ate a spoonful of soil
so I chewed a worm.

She ate half a worm
so I had two whole slugs.

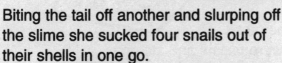

Biting the tail off another and slurping off
the slime she sucked four snails out of
their shells in one go.

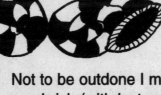

Not to be outdone I made a frogspawn
sandwich (with last week's bread) and
bit into it twice.

She snatched it off me, added three caterpillars,
a handful of ants, a bumble bee and carried on
munching.

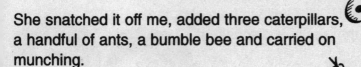

I went and took a great big gulp from the dog's water bowl.
She went and took a great big mouthful of dog food.

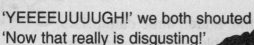

I told her that the rabbit
    droppings were raisins and ate one
so she got a shovelful and gobbled them all up.

I was just about to mash up a
    cowpat into a stew
when Dad came outside and
    shouted us in for tea.

'What's for tea?' asked my sister.
'Liver and cabbage" shouted Dad.

'YEEEEUUUUGH!' we both shouted
'Now that really is disgusting!'

Paul Cookson

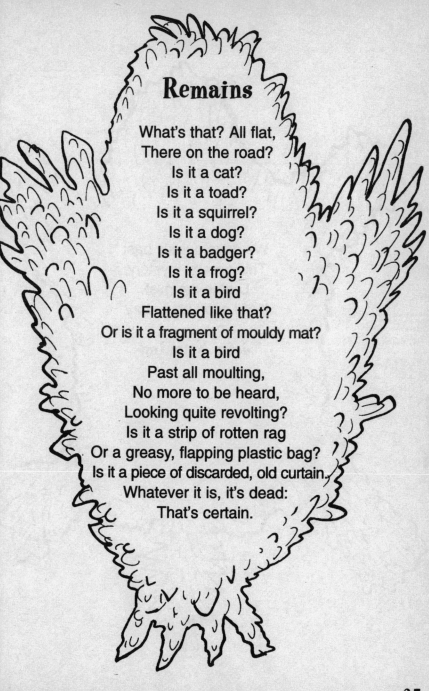

Remains

What's that? All flat,
There on the road?
Is it a cat?
Is it a toad?
Is it a squirrel?
Is it a dog?
Is it a badger?
Is it a frog?
Is it a bird
Flattened like that?
Or is it a fragment of mouldy mat?
Is it a bird
Past all moulting,
No more to be heard,
Looking quite revolting?
Is it a strip of rotten rag
Or a greasy, flapping plastic bag?
Is it a piece of discarded, old curtain,
Whatever it is, it's dead:
That's certain.

We drive quickly past
This grubby mystery.
Lost in the mist,
It will soon be history.

John Kitching

Nursery Rhymes

Spotty Lottie, gruesome, grotty,
How does your garden grow?

    With blood-sucking shrubs
    Slimy with slugs
    All eager to savage your toe!

Mary had a vampire bat,
Its fangs were sharp as tin
And the blood it sucked out of her neck
Went dribbling down its chin!

Matt Simpson

Dinner on Elm Street

Thrice the old school cat hath spewed.
Teachers shriek and children whine:
Ring the bell! 'Tis time! 'Tis time!

Round about the cauldron go,
In the mouldy cabbage throw,
Stone-cold custard, thick with lumps,
Germs from Kevin (sick with mumps).
Boil up sprouts for greenish smell,
Add sweaty stock, cheese pie as well.

Froth and splutter, boil and bubble.
March them in here at the double.

Fillet of an ancient steak
In the cauldron boil and bake.
Eye of spud and spawn of frog,
A chocolate moose, a heated dog.
Add the goo from 'twixt the toes
And crusty bits from round the
    nose.

Froth and splutter, boil and bubble.
March them in here at the double.

Lumpy mincemeat, grey and gristly,
Giblets, gizzards, all things grizzly.
Beak of chicken in a nugget,
With greasy chips the kids will love it.
Scab of knee sprinkle in,
Squeeze juice of pimple from a chin
Here's the spell to make you thinner.
It's the nightmare Elm Street dinner.

Froth and splutter, boil and bubble.
March them in here at the double!

Michaela Morgan

Choosing Schools

Why did you send your son to our school?
Was it the teachers you liked, or the rules?
Was it the classrooms, the playground, the pool?
Why did you send your son to our school?

We liked your staff, the library, the hall,
But, Sir, that wasn't the reason at all.
My son has the runniest nose ever seen,
So I chose the school for its uniform – green.

Angi Holden

Fido Has Died, Oh

When I discovered Fido was dead
I dug a hole behind the shed.
Shedding tears, that stained my face,
I laid my dog in his last resting place.

Without my pet, life didn't seem right,
So I dug him up the other night.
I figured that if I used my brain
I could make my Fido live again.

So, I took a trolley and removed the wheels
And screwed them to my dead dog's heels.
An elastic band wrapped round a nail,
Attached to my finger, wagged his tail.
I placed a tape in the throat of my hound
Which made an authentic doggie sound.

We go for walks o'er fields and parks;
He follows me; he wags; he barks.
I tell him to sit and he obeys.
If I say 'stay' – well – he stays.

He doesn't need feeding, he doesn't have fleas;
He doesn't mess on pavements or cock his leg by trees.
He must be healthy, as he never needs the vet.
We'll always be together – me and my perfect pet.

John Coldwell

Revenge of the Man-eating Gerbils

Be Afraid, Be Very Afraid

'Nothing tastes quite like a gerbil',
someone once wrote, in a book.
So, rodents have teamed-up together;
surprises in store, for the cook.

The SGS* and gangster hamsters,
are sharpening fangs. Here's the plan:
as revenge for 'a gerbil with salad',
they've decided to dine – on Man!

Gnawing kneecaps and nibbling nostrils;
jellied elbows, small mammals are salting.
Rodents rise-up, save your cousins.
The gerbils are really revolting.

*Special Gerbil Squadron

Mike Johnson

Archie

I once had a hamster called Archie
Which I kept in a cage in my room.
His habits were mostly nocturnal,
His wheel whirred away in the gloom.

Through the day he slept silently curled
In a nest box, soft cotton wool lined,
Having first filled the corners with food –
Apple and things of that kind.

Our cat would patiently watch him,
Tail twitching to show her frustration,
Or scratch at his cage with her claws
Overcome with delicious temptation.

Sometimes, when firmly reminded,
I'd reluctantly clean Archie's home.
On one such occasion the creature
Decided to go for a roam.

Try as I might to recapture
My hamster, he got clean away.
I finally gave up the search –
Friends called, I went out to play.

Days later I was in deep trouble,
When Mum tidied under my bed.
Amongst board games and slippers and comics
She came across Archibald's head.

Angi Holden

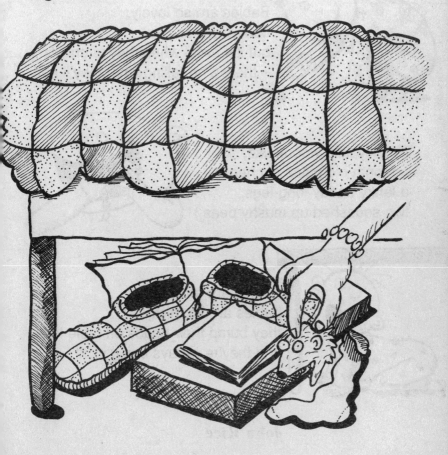

Babies are so . . .

Babies are so pretty,
babies are so sweet,
but it's awful when they're crawling
and can't quite use their feet.

Babies are so lovely,
babies are so neat,
but it's awful when they're crawling
– there's no telling what they'll eat!

(A juicy little woodlouse,
a month-old piece of cheese,
a lanky daddy-long-legs,
two squashed up mushy peas.)

Babies are so yeuchy,
babies are so thick,
they bump their heads on table legs
and they're always being sick!

John Rice

Gnash
(for Emma, Julie and Lily)

All right, I've got bad teeth
don't tell me again
OK so they're yellow at the edges and
one of them is amazingly squint and
there's an interesting collection of metal and
the gums are wearing down and
yes I know they're like that thank you
but no it wasn't eating too many sweeties did it
when I was young we sucked rusty railings instead of
    lollipops
but if you keep trying to empty the penny tray
maybe the dentist will be able to make you a set every
    bit as nice;
and anyway they've been in my mouth a long long time
twenty times longer than yours. They've chewed on life,
    these teeth,
and they're still my own, still strong and sharp,
and you won't be looking at them
when they bite into your neck.

Dave Calder

My Mates

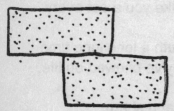

Jimmy Greenwood kisses slugs.
I've seen him.
He'll let you look for 50p.
He puts one on his hand
pushes out his lips
shuts his eyes (nearly)
and lays a smacker on its face.
When he pulls his lips away
they're covered in slime
and he licks it off.

He loves them.
If he could, he'd marry a slug.
One of the big fat black ones
or the long, streaky brown ones.

He calls them 'darling'
'dearest' and 'sweetie pie'.
I've heard him.
It's only 20p to listen.
He puts his mouth right up
to where he thinks their ear is
and whispers.

He even takes them to bed with him.
He puts them inside his 'jamas
and lets them slither over his belly.
So he says.

I've got 20p left.
I'm off to watch Alan Wright
push woodlice up his nose.

Gus Grenfell

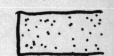

Fresh on the Menu Tonight

How do you fancy
eating a frog –
not just the legs,
the whole hog?

Uncooked, of course,
wet from the pond;
its podgy gold eyes
staring you out
as you lift it
to your mouth.

Imagine
the feel of the skin,
the soft, meaty flesh
as you sink
your teeth in
– and think
of those dangling
back legs and webbed toes
frantically thrashing
and punching fresh air,
trying to get
a grip on your chin

And its last
desperate croak
as
it
s
l
i
p
s
down your throat!

Pat Leighton

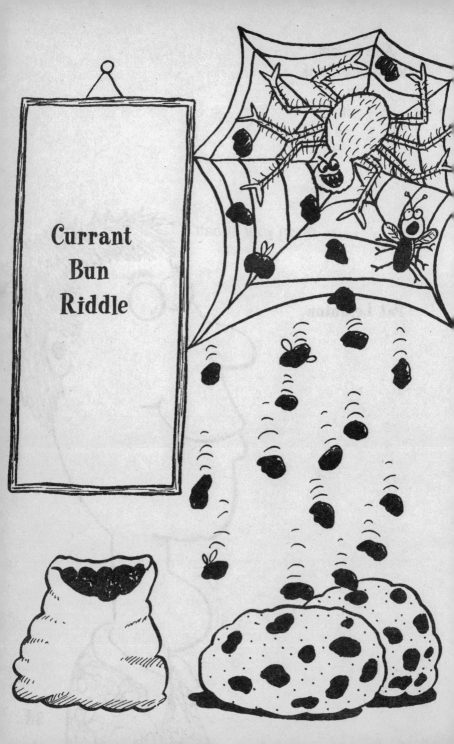

Currant
Bun
Riddle

Dead flies are collected
by spiders and things,
who chew up their bodies
and crunch at their wings.

Before spitting them out
in bundles of black,
to sell them to bakers
for ten pence a pack.

So next time you buy
a big currant bun,
remember the hard work
put into each one.

Andrew Collett

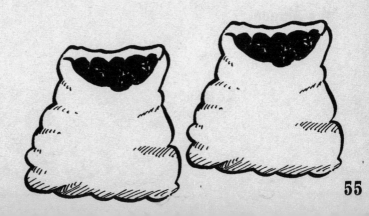

Rover

All the guests have gone home,
home to Deal, Diss and Dover.
Our house looks like a tip
now the party is over.
Time to call in our hound,
rough and ravenous Rover.

He devours all the scraps
cast aside by the ravers:
sausage ends, curried rice,
and crushed crisps of all flavours.
Rover wolfs down the lot:
kebabs, kumquats, and Quavers.

That dog's a devourer,
he's our household improver.
Prawns, peanuts and prunes gulped
by our rubbish remover.
Rover's tongue sweeps each rug:
he's one huge, hairy hoover.

Wes Magee

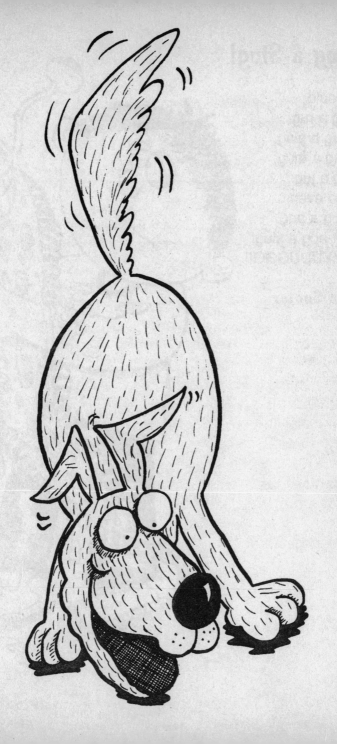

Hug a Slug!

I could
tug a rug,
glug a plug,
slug a thug,
lug a jug
and even
mug a bug
but hug a slug!
YYYUUUGGG!!

Ian Souter

Let's Face It

'You're dirty, disgustingly dirty',
My mother used to cry,
Ordering me to sit.
Then she wiped the chocolate from my face
With her handkerchief
Covered with spit!

John Kitching

NOTHING TASTES QUITE LIKE A GERBIL

**and other vile verses
chosen by David Orme**

Nothing Tastes Quite Like a Gerbil

Nothing tastes quite like a gerbil

They're small and tasty to eat –

Morsels of sweet rodent protein

From whiskers to cute little feet!

You can bake them, roast them or fry them,

They grill nicely and you can have them *en croûte*,

In garlic butter they're simply delicious

You can even serve them with fruit.

So you can keep your beef and your chicken,

Your lamb and your ham on the bone,

I'll have gerbil as my daily diet

And what's more – I can breed them at home!

Tony Langham